Every new generation of children is enthralled by the famous stories in our Well-Loved Tales series. Younger ones love to have the stories read to them. Older children enjoy the exciting stories in an easy-to-read text.

LADYBIRD BOOKS, INC.
Lewiston, Maine 04240 U.S.A.
© LADYBIRD BOOKS LTD MCMLXXXVI
Loughborough, Leicestershire, England

Printed in England

The Little Red Hen

retold for easy reading
by VERA SOUTHGATE
illustrated by STEPHEN HOLMES

Ladybird Books

Once upon a time, there was a little red hen who lived in a farmyard.

One day the little red hen
found some grains of wheat.

She took them to the other
animals in the farmyard.

"Who will help me plant these grains of wheat?" asked the little red hen.

"Not I," said the cat.

"Not I," said the rat.

"Not I," said the pig.

"Then I will plant the grains
myself," said the little red hen.

So she did.

Every day the little red hen went to the field to watch the grains of wheat growing.

They grew tall and strong.

One day, the little red hen
saw that the wheat was ready
to be cut.

So she went to the other
animals in the farmyard.

"Who will help me cut the
wheat?" asked the little
red hen.

"Not I," said the cat.

"Not I," said the rat.

"Not I," said the pig.

"Then I will cut the wheat myself," said the little red hen.

So she did.

"Now the wheat is ready to be made into flour," said the little red hen to herself, as she set off for the farmyard.

"Who will help me take the
wheat to the mill, to be ground
into flour?" asked the little
red hen.

"Not I," said the cat.

"Not I," said the rat.

"Not I," said the pig.

"Then I will take the wheat to
the mill myself," said the little
red hen.

So she did.

The little red hen took the
wheat to the mill, and the
miller ground it into flour.

When the wheat had been
ground into flour, the little red
hen took it to the other animals
in the farmyard.

"Who will help me take this
flour to the baker, to be made
into bread?" asked the little
red hen.

"Not I," said the cat.

"Not I," said the rat.

"Not I," said the pig.

"Then I will take the flour to the baker myself," said the little red hen.

So she did.

The little red hen took the
flour to the baker, and the
baker made it into bread.

43

When the bread was baked, the
little red hen took it to the
other animals in the farmyard.

45

"Now the bread is ready to be eaten," said the little red hen. "Who will help me eat the bread?"

"I will," said the cat.

"I will," said the rat.

"I will," said the pig.

"No, you will not," said the little red hen. "I will eat it myself."

So she did.

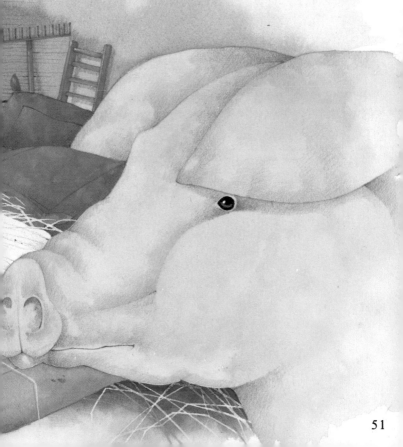